BEYOND EQUESTRIA

RAINBOW DASH
RIGHTS THE SHIP

Little, Brown and Company
Hachette Book Group
1290 Avenue of the Americas, New York, NY 10104
Visit us at LBYR.com
mylittlepony.com

First Edition: February 2018

Little, Brown and Company is a division of Hachette Book Group, Inc. The Little, Brown name and logo are trademarks of Hachette Book Group, Inc.

The publisher is not responsible for websites (or their content) that are not owned by the publisher.

Library of Congress Control Number 2017957396

ISBNs: 978-0-316-55752-8 (paper over board), 978-0-316-55749-8 (ebook)

Printed in the United States of America

LSC-C

10 9 8 7 6 5 4 3 2 1

BEYOND EQUESTRIA

RAINBOW DASH RIGHTS THE SHIP

G. M. Berrow

Little, Brown and Company
New York • Boston

CHAPTER ONE

On a normal day, Rainbow Dash would have barely noticed the sunlight peeking through the curtains of her bedroom. But this was not a normal day, and this was not her bedroom. At least, it wasn't *anymore*. Rainbow Dash was back in her hometown of Cloudsdale. Instead of nestling into her fluffy cloud duvet back above Ponyville, the blue Pegasus was tucked tightly into the rainbow-patterned sheets of her fillyhood bed. She had a wing cramp. Clearly the bed was much smaller than she'd remembered.

Rainbow Dash yawned and watched as the light made its way across the eclectic array of trophies, ribbons, and relics of her youth that were still in the exact spots they had been years ago when she'd carefully arranged and rearranged them with her tiny hooves. There were so many memories on display!

Rainbow Dash's eyes landed on her bookshelf, where her old stuffed teddy bear, Blue-Blue, sat with his signature blank expression. Rainbow Dash instantly remembered when her mother had given him to her as a reward for being brave through her first dentist appointment. Rainbow Dash then noticed her cloud-rimmed basketball hoop and recalled all the hours she had spent perfecting the perfect shot instead of completing her homework assignments. She never did enjoy studying too much. Only one test had ever mattered to Rainbow Dash—the one to get into the Wonderbolts!

The poster above the hoop was evidence of Rainbow Dash's longstanding devotion to the elite Pegasus flight team. It depicted the renowned Wonderbolt Super Stream in action—wings outspread and racing toward the big finish in the famous "Eye of the Storm" routine. It was a legendary show! Young Rainbow Dash had stared at that poster as she drifted off to sleep each night, dreaming of the day when she, too, would become a Wonderbolt and don the blue-and-yellow flight suit.

Now that her dream had finally come true, Rainbow Dash often found herself visiting locales across Equestria with her team, performing complex routines and thrilling feats to the delight of adoring onlookers. Which was precisely why she was back here at this very moment, in Cloudsdale, in her parents' house.

"Good morning, dearest Dashie-kins!" Windy Whistles burst into the bedroom, carrying a tray of steaming porridge and toast slathered with cloudberry jam. The cup of orange juice sloshed around as Windy practically shook with excitement at hosting her daughter. "I made your favorite brekkie! How's *my* favorite little Wonderbolt feeling today?!"

"I'm, uh—" Rainbow could barely stammer before her dad, Bow Hothoof, popped in behind her mom.

"Is she up yet, dear? Is our champion daughter ready for her big debut in the Wonderbolts'

anniversary show—The Loopy Woop Woop?!"
He peered over Windy's shoulder with a gigantic smile spreading across his violet face. His
rainbow mane poked out in every direction,
just like his daughter's.

"Dad, it's *called* the Loop-de-Loop Hoopla."
Rainbow Dash sighed with a smirk as she bolted
upright in bed. "And I guess I'm up now." She
tossed the covers away and began to climb out.

"No, no! Don't move a muscle, missy," Windy
urged as she rushed over and tucked her daughter back in, balancing the breakfast tray in an
impressive teetering display. "Relax and eat
your food. You need to save your energy for
the big performance. Everypony in Cloudsdale is coming, and they just can't wait to see
you! The girls are even coming—making a
whole day of it! Dressing up, seeing the show,

then grabbing lunch afterward at the Rain-drop Café. Finally, it's *my* turn to show off my daughter. If I hear another thing about Snow-fall's daughter, Moon Trotter, and her Snow-flake awards, I just don't know!"

"The *giiirls*?" Rainbow groaned. "All of them?" Rainbow's mother was very active in the Cloudsdale Decorative Plate Collecting Club. It sounded tame enough, but when all those mares got together, they could be quite the hoof-ful.

"No, no, of course not." Windy laughed. "That would be ridiculous! Just Snowfall, Blue Skies, Pom Pom, Dew Shine, Sparkle Showers, Sunny Shores, and…Helen." Windy grinned proudly. "Oh! And Barbara."

"Who doesn't love Barbara?" Rainbow Dash laughed nervously and hid her mounting feelings of anxiety by taking a bite of toast. Ever since she'd blown up at her parents for being too supportive at her last Wonderbolts show, Rainbow Dash had made a serious effort to accept their support and praise. She was a lucky pony to have such loving parents, even if they were over-the-top sometimes. Thanks to Scootaloo and her school report, Rainbow Dash remembered that now.

"And I hope it's okay that I invited the old buckball team, too," Bow Hothoof added, blushing. "They still can't believe that the little tyke who used to fly around the court following 'em and asking 'em to race is a real Wonderbolt now!" Bow wiped away a proud tear. He gathered Rainbow Dash into a big bear hug.

"Invite the whole city, if ya want. I actually invited some friends, too," Rainbow Dash admitted. "But I'm really not sure if they're going to come. I mean—I don't even know if they got my invitation...."

"Why wouldn't they?" Windy furrowed her brow. "Didn't you have their addresses?"

"It's not really like that," Rainbow explained, taking the last bite of porridge. She wiped away a rogue drop from her chin. "They, uh...don't have addresses. These friends are sort of...always on the go? I hope it's okay—I kinda invited them to the house first."

"How lovely!" Windy chirped with her signature optimism. "It's so nice to have guests."

"Well, I can't wait to meet 'em," Bow Hothoof commented. "Any friend of my daughter's is welcome in this home. Now, how about you let me do a bit of tidying before they arrive?" He trotted over to the window and thrust the curtains open. A blast of fresh air and sunlight filled the room. But before Rainbow Dash could thank her dad, Bow let out a loud, startled grunt.

"Whoa!" Bow's jaw dropped and his eyes became larger than a set of Windy Whistle's collector plates. "What in the cumulonimbus is that?!"

"Stand back!" Rainbow Dash sprang to action and darted over. She was ready to take on whatever fearsome sight she might discover. Rainbow Dash wasn't afraid. She'd seen it all: Dragons, Manticores, new and scary creatures in Klugetown, and even a Storm King.

That's why Rainbow Dash should have expected to see the massive object lurching straight toward their house.

But it took her completely by surprise.

CHAPTER TWO

The colossal airship burst into view with its colorful feathered wing-sails outspread, cutting through the wispy clouds. It felt like forever since Rainbow Dash had seen her new friends, Captain Celaeno and the swashbuckling pirate parrot crew, but there they were—right in front of her parents' house! It almost didn't seem real.

"It's them!" Rainbow Dash shouted with

glee as the quickening breeze picked up and whooshed through the window and into her mane. "My friends are here!" She spun around to see that the color was coming back to Bow's and Windy's faces as they breathed a sigh of relief. It had been such a long time since they'd been introduced to friends of their daughter. But ever since they'd become privy to the information that Rainbow Dash was a Wonderbolt, it was as if their social circle was widening tenfold.

"Well, what are you waiting for, dear?" Windy called out over the loud hum of the ship outside. Her cropped red-orange mane whipped against her forehead in the wind. "Ask them in!"

Rainbow Dash darted to the yard, speeding past her mother's prized hydro-rangea bushes and across the perfectly manicured mist lawn. As the ship's massive balloon approached, it seemed to fill up the whole sky, eclipsing the golden sun and shrouding the family home in darkness for a brief moment.

It was easy to spot the outline of Captain Celaeno, a tall parrot with white and green feathers, by the distinctive shape of her wide-brimmed pirate's hat with the peach plume. She stood triumphantly at the bow of the ship, poised with her claws on her hips. Her crew of birds flocked and squawked around her. They tightened ropes and pulled pulleys to ready the ship for docking. Once they'd met with solid cloud and thrown down their chains, the crew birds lowered the gangplank.

"Rainbow Dash!" Captain Celaeno shouted,

her beak twisting into a sneaky grin. "You sent for us?"

"This is . . . *awesome!*" Rainbow Dash squeaked in delight as she zoomed over. "Boy, are you guys a sight for sore eyes! I can't believe my letter made it you." Rainbow Dash put her hoof to her chin and raised her brow, remembering the way Fluttershy had tied the note to a bird's little foot and sent it off into the sky. "That random homing pigeon Fluttershy found to deliver it must have been a genius. . . ."

"Actually"—Captain Celaeno laughed as she began walking down the gangplank—"that was Putt-Putt. Used to be a part of the crew." She winked at Rainbow Dash, who couldn't tell if the captain was joking or not.

"Rainbow Dash!" called out a green parrot with an eye patch and wild red head feathers.

He looked around in awe at the impressive neighborhood built entirely out of cloud structures. "This is where you live?"

"No, First Mate Mullet." Rainbow Dash shook her head. She motioned to the scenery behind her with pride. "This is where I grew up! Welcome to Cloudsdale—the Pegasus city. Cool, huh?"

"*Almost* as cool as where we hatched back in Ornithia," Mullet admitted as he ambled down after the giggling captain. The other pirates followed suit: the burly and hook-clawed Boyle, the boisterous Lix Spittle, and the wacky cross-eyed shipmate, Squabble. The pirate birds were clearly as excited to see Rainbow Dash as she was to see them! So why did they stop abruptly at the bottom of the wooden plank and stare at one another? Even Boyle looked nervous.

Rainbow Dash cocked her head and her spiky mane flipped to the side. "Everything okay?" She looked to her mother for any clues. Was it true that birds needed extra encouragement to jump from their nests and spread their wings? Windy just shrugged and did what any good mother would do—started cheering them on.

"Dashie is right—don't be shy now! You can do it! Get on down here and let us host you ladies and gentlebirds!" Windy Whistles hollered, accidentally startling Squabble. The batty bird squawked and flapped his feathered arms, knocking over Lix Spittle, who came tumbling down the gangplank, shrieking. She grabbed on to the wood with all her claws, eyes bulging out of her head.

"Sorry about them, ma'am," Celaeno replied

with a sigh. "Rainbow Dash's letter *may* have mentioned that only Pegasus ponies can walk on the clouds here. These scalawags are being a bit…er…*dramatic* about it. Not to worry, though!" Captain Celaeno tugged at two straps on her shoulders and spun around to reveal a contraption that looked like a mini-balloon with jets. "We bartered for these sky-packs from a friendly Earth pony aeronaut on the way here!" She tugged at the straps again and soared over, landing her claws safely on the cloud lawn next to Rainbow Dash.

Rainbow Dash leaned in to get better look at the unique contraption. "Okay, these are seriously cool," she admitted with a nod of approval. All the other times her non-Pegasus friends had visited Cloudsdale were thanks to seriously complicated spells placed on them by

Twilight Sparkle. Rainbow Dash made a mental note to get some of these snazzy sky-packs to keep on hoof for her Ponyville friends.

While First Mate Mullet anchored the ship to the side of Rainbow Dash's house, Boyle helped the others figure out how to work their packs. Soon, the whole crew of pirates began jumping across the clouds in a sort of bouncy motion and giggling like fillies and colts. As Captain Celaeno and Rainbow Dash stood together watching the madness of the ragtag crew, Windy Whistles rushed over in a panic. "If we don't leave soon, we're going to be late to the Wonderbolts' Hoopla!"

"Oh no!" Celaeno cried. She didn't want to make Rainbow Dash tardy for the very event that they had come all this way to see. "You'd better get a move on, matey."

"Oh, right. Well, at least we know they can't start without me, huh?" Rainbow Dash joked before taking off at full speed toward Wonderbolts Stadium. "See ya there, scalawags!"

Bow Hothoof grinned at the signature rainbow trail his daughter left in the sky. This was going to be an excellent performance, and he couldn't wait for Rainbow Dash's new friends to see just how special she was. "Hurry, everybird! We've got a show to get to."

CHAPTER THREE

The second after the Loop-de-Loop Hoopla show had concluded, there was already a crowd of adoring pony fans gathered around Rainbow Dash. Apparently, she was famous. Captain Celaeno and her crew tried to hang back and let all the ponies have their turn, but the pirates couldn't help but rush over and push through the crowd to congratulate her.

They had never seen such a spectacle in all

their lives! Except perhaps the moment in which Rainbow Dash and her friends had convinced them to stop working for the Storm King and be awesome again. But even the Sonic Rainboom she'd performed back then didn't hold a candle to the expert flight patterns of the Wonderbolts performing together as a team.

"That was incredible!" Captain Celaeno gushed. She threw her feathered arms up in the air to illustrate the maneuver. "That loopy thing that ended in a giant, pony firework? We knew you had moves, but not like that."

"Nice job, kid." Boyle gave her a friendly nudge. "I wasn't sure this whole flying pony show thing would be worth leaving our swashbuckling schedule for, but I'm glad the captain made us come check it out."

"Come on, I'd never steer you wrong," joked

Captain Celaeno. "Well, at least not again, I won't." Their Storm King days were long over. Now Celaeno made sure that she and her crew were chasing nothing but adventure. And friendship from time to time.

"Thanks, guys." Rainbow Dash peeled off her yellow-and-blue Wonderbolts mask. "It means a lot to me that you would take time off and support my little show." She blushed pink with embarrassment. Rainbow Dash had performed with the Wonderbolts a hundred times by now, but for some reason knowing that all these supercool pirates had just witnessed it made her feel a bit silly. She had to make the journey they'd taken all the way to Cloudsdale from Celestia-knows-where worth their while. An idea began to form in her head.

"Hey, Captain!" Rainbow Dash blurted out.

"While you're here, how about I show you birds around Cloudsdale?"

"A tour of the sights?" First Mate Mullet adjusted his eye patch and grinned. "I do love me a good guided tour! Whaddya say, Boyle?"

"Sure." Boyle grunted and pointed his hook at the towering Weather Factory building in the distance. "Can we see what's inside that, there?"

"Does it include dinner?" Lix Spittle grunted. That old cook always had food on her bird brain. "Don't forget—we fed you and your friends our finest slop aboard the old ship!"

Rainbow Dash cringed at the memory. The friends they made onboard Celaeno's ship had been great, but the cuisine was something she'd rather forget. The taste of the powdery gray gruel hadn't left her taste buds for weeks after. She'd eaten probably thirty cupcakes, which Pinkie Pie had been happy to make, to try to get rid of it.

"Why, of course—we've got plenty of food at home," Windy Whistles interjected before Rainbow Dash could open her mouth. "I went shopping at the Supercloud 9 in preparation for our dear Dashie's visit." Windy leaned in to Lix Spittle and lowered her voice. "Our little athlete has always had the appetite of a grown stallion...."

"Are you sure, Mom?" said Rainbow Dash, ignoring the comment. "I bet these guys want to try one of Cloudsdale's fancy restaurants or something...."

"Horsefeathers! How does a fresh batch of

pasta-and-potato sandwiches on sourdough sound?" Bow Hothoof added, raising his eyebrows at Rainbow Dash. Her parents knew if there was one thing she couldn't resist, it was her favorite, carb-loaded food. As a filly, she had practically refused to eat anything else.

"I've never even *heard* of that...." Captain Celaeno scratched her feathered chin and considered. The crew leaned in, waiting for the bird's official word. "Which means...it's a brand-new adventure—a *food* adventure. Onward to pasta-and-potato sandwiches!" She put one claw on her hip and pointed the other in the direction of Rainbow Dash's house. The pirates cheered and Rainbow Dash's parents joined in, leading the way to the kitchen.

Later, as she looked around the house brimming with family and new friends, Rainbow Dash felt her heart filling up with happiness. Now all she had to do was fill up her tummy, too.

CHAPTER FOUR

The band of scalawags scurried through the swirling, misty streets of Cloudsdale, looking quite out of place. At every place they'd visited so far—the Weather Factory, the shopping district, and even Pegasus Park—the local ponies had gawked and whispered at the curious sight of a bunch of giant birds wearing pirate getups and sky-packs. If it weren't for their pony tour guides, the crew might have caused quite the panic in the streets. Luckily, Windy Whistles and Bow Hothoof were very trustworthy and well liked. And they knew almost everypony in town.

"Hello, Barbara!" Windy shouted as she waved to a very confused yellow Pegasus wearing a string of pearls. "Hope you enjoyed the Hoopla!" Barbara sized up the birds and balked, scrunching up her muzzle. Then she nodded politely and flew off. The prim pony looked over her shoulder five times before disappearing around the corner. Windy Whistles sighed in defeat.

"So, Captain—where to next?" Mullet grunted as he unfolded the souvenir map of the city he'd bought at a kiosk. He held the paper up close to his good eyeball. "The Snowfall Ice Cream Stop or the Pop-Pop-Popsicle Shop?"

"I have an even better idea!" Bow Hothoof

exclaimed, coming to a screeching halt at the corner of Weatherwood and Vane streets. The birds followed suit, knocking into one another like a row of dominoes. But thanks to their sky-packs, they didn't tumble to the ground. They just bounced off each other like balloons.

"What's better than ice cream?" Lix Spittle wondered aloud. A chorus of sounds from the rest of the crew made it clear that they were racking their brains for the same answer.

"Priceless relics of the past worth lots of bits?" Bow Hothoof puffed up his chest, proud of his brilliant idea. But the birds just stared back at him with blank expressions. Bow sighed. Clearly he had to spell it out for them. "You know . . . *treasure!*"

"Why didn't you say so sooner, mate?!" Captain Celaeno floated over, put her claw on

Bow's shoulder, and gave a little wink to Rainbow Dash. She turned to her crew. "Whoever wants to find treasure instead of ice cream, say 'aye'!"

"*AYE!*" the birds cheered, all of them pumping their right claws in the air with glee (except for Boyle, who lifted his hook).

"Yeah! I mean—aye!" Rainbow Dash echoed, getting into the pirate spirit. She couldn't imagine what treasure her dad was referring to, but she hoped it wasn't just her mom's plate collection or his trophy from the Buckball Intramural Championships. That would be super embarrassing.

"Then follow me, you, er...scalawags!" Bow commanded proudly.

Windy giggled at her husband's attempt to sound like a pirate. "Nice one, honey."

After a few blocks following Bow Hothoof

and singing a silly pirate's sky shanty called "Treasure Weather," the crew stopped in front of a beautiful building. It had regal yet sturdy columns made of thick cloud evenly spaced along the facade. A string of glittering, decorative stars dotted around the gigantic double doors. Two statues of Pegasi flanked the wide steps leading to the top.

"Da-*aaaad*," Rainbow Dash groaned. "You brought us to the Cloudsdale History Museum?" She only remembered it from her class field trips as the most boring place ever.

"What? They seem to be excited!" Bow pointed to the steps, which were now occupied by the horde of birds all trying to race one another to the top. Scared ponies darted out of the way.

"Oh dear." Windy Whistles laughed. "Looks

like we've got some history buffs on our hooves."
Bow and Windy began the ascent up the stairs,
but Rainbow Dash zoomed past them.

"Hey, guys, wait up!" Rainbow Dash hollered to the pirates. Maybe she could make the
museum seem little bit cooler if she explained
some of the exhibits. She soared into the open
doors to head them off. But it was too late!
The pirates had already split up and spread out
across the building, searching the rooms for the
alleged treasure. What had Bow done?

+ + + + +

Over in the ancient armory room, Lix Spittle
had already found something shiny. "What's
this, eh?" Lix knocked her claw on the glass
case so hard it nearly shattered. She squashed
her beak against the case for a better look. "A

shield or something? Could be worth some-thin'..." She scratched at the seams of the case to try to see how easy it would be to lift the lid off.

"Don't touch that, Lix! That's *Netitus*!" Rainbow Dash urged as she pulled the pink-feathered pirate away from the priceless artifact. "Flash Magnus's fireproof shield? The one he used to save his fellow Legionnaires from the Dragon's lair?"

Lix shrugged with an annoyed grunt. She'd never heard the legend of the Cloudsdale hero Flash Magnus and didn't seem to want to. "So?"

"So, we have to leave it here." Rainbow Dash sighed, realizing that this wasn't going to be the end of the discussion. Across the room, Boyle was sizing up an old jewelry box from the pre-Equestrian era. Several of the other pirates in the grand museum room had fixated on items in cases and were trying to figure out how to steal them as well.

"We have to leave everything in here alone! These treasures are not for the taking . . . just for admiring. They're all really important parts of Pegasus history!" Rainbow Dash paused. How could she make them understand why they couldn't just barge in, smash the glass, and take the pretty, shiny objects? "Do you want to hear some stories about 'em?"

CHAPTER FIVE

Why not?" Captain Celaeno shouted. "Spin us a yarn, Dash!" She hobbled over, the sound of her emerald peg leg echoing on the marbled floor. At the sign of their captain retreating from the glass cases, the others quickly abandoned their posts. They gathered around a very relieved Rainbow Dash.

"So which item are you curious about?" Rainbow Dash flew over to a giant pair of scissors. "The very ribbon-cutting scissors that the mayor used to open Town Hall? Or how about Commander Easyglider's original flight jacket?" She gestured to a ponnequin wearing an aviator-style jacket with fluffy lapels and patches all over it.

"What can you tell us about *that* one?" Celaeno's eyes flashed with excitement as she motioned to the most inconspicuous display of them all, tucked away in the darkest corner of the room. A huge deep-red gem rotated slowly in a glass orb. Its jagged edges sparkled under the expertly placed display lights. The pirates' eyes bulged with desire. They ambled across the museum, pushing one another out of the way to behold its beauty up close.

A couple of ponies who'd been admiring the gem scampered away from the exhibit, letting the pirates have their turn. Even the museum docent stepped back after he saw the sheer size of Boyle. Rainbow Dash knew that her pirate friends weren't trying to scare anypony, but they could be very intimidating. Maybe it was best for her to quickly tell them the story of the gem so they could all hightail it out of there. They could go back to her parents' house and play pony charades or something instead.

"Aye, Captain, she's a beaut!" cooed Mullet, tugging at his red bandana and practically salivating. "It's the biggest ruby I've ever seen!"

"Actually, it's a garnet. The Good Fortune Garnet to be exact!" Rainbow Dash explained. She landed between the gem and the pirates, forcing them to take a few steps back from the display. "Long, long ago, back when Cloudsdale was founded, Pegasi came from all over the world to bring gifts to the new settlement. This super-mysterious and totally powerful Alicorn brought this gem, claiming that it would help the ponies to always be super happy and have cool stuff happen to them! Anyway, ever since then, Pegasus legend has it that the Good Fortune Garnet will bring luck to anypony—or any city, I guess—that has it."

Windy and Bow, who had been busy reading a display on ancient ceremonial weather practices, came trotting over to join the discussion. "It really is quite stunning, isn't it?" Windy Whistles marveled.

"Yup." Rainbow Dash sighed and motioned to the gem. "Too bad this one here's just a glass replica of the real thing, right, Mom?" At this, a collective audible gasp escaped the beaks of the pirates.

"That's correct," Windy confirmed. Bow Hothoof backed her up with a nod.

"Wait—where's the original?" Captain Celaeno prodded. She couldn't tear her eyes away from the replica gem, so she could hardly imagine how amazing the real thing must be. She felt a sudden urge to make it hers. But where could it be? Surely there had to be some sort of clue in Cloudsdale.

"It was stolen years ago...." Rainbow Dash shrugged. "Though back in school we all used to joke that we'd find it one day and be the heroes of Cloudsdale! One of my teachers was really into it. He even helped me draw this treasure map, claiming that the gem was some-where inside the Thunder Jungle."

"A treasure map?" Celaeno's heart quick-ened. She could feel it—adventure calling! She never used to believe in gems that were cursed or magically enhanced to bring good luck, but after the mysterious green crystal known as the Misfortune Malachite found its way onto their ship, Captain Celaeno had reconsidered her stance. "Do you still have it, Rainbow Dash? Can you find the map?"

"That was really long time ago. Probably not—"

"Of course we do!" Windy chirped, a smile taking over her freckled cheeks. "I can show you exactly where it is back at the house. Aren't you so glad I keep *everything*?"

CHAPTER SIX

There was a flurry of activity as soon as the pirates boarded their airship again. A ton of work had to be done to ready the vessel for a new journey. Aside from Squabble's duty swabbing the poop deck, the crew had to clean the feathered sails, restock Lix's galley with fresh food and supplies, and fill the balloon with hot air. Captain Celaeno set straight to work, barking orders at her shipmates and doing routine quality checks of every inch of the precious boat. Practically the only good thing that had come out of their time working for the Storm King's fleet was the strict and streamlined routine of their ship's upkeep.

"I can't believe you convinced me to go with you to try to chase the Good Fortune Garnet!" Rainbow Dash laughed. She trudged up the gangplank, feeling the heavy weight of the saddlebag her mother had packed for her. It had about ten pasta-and-potato sandwiches on sourdough inside, along with the scribbly treasure map from her school days. "Pretty much every Pegasus says that it's only a schoolpony myth."

"Wouldn't you like to know for sure, though?" Captain Celaeno reached her claw out and hoisted Rainbow Dash onto the deck. "Imagine being the pony who finds the garnet!"

In truth, the idea of returning the gem to Cloudsdale after hundreds of years did give Rainbow Dash a twinge of excitement.

"Yeah, I guess it would be pretty cool," she admitted, picturing the ceremony in which they replaced the fake gem with the real one. "But it still doesn't mean that the legend is real."

"But your adventurer friend might know, right?" Celaeno climbed up the steps that led to the ship's steering wheel. She removed her hat to smooth down her head feathers. "What's her name again?"

"Daring Do," Rainbow Dash answered. "If anypony knows something about the Good Fortune Garnet, it's definitely her."

Though it felt awesome to be setting out on a journey with her new friends, Rainbow Dash began to grow nervous. Daring Do wasn't the type of pony who loved big crowds of visitors showing up at her door, let alone random visitors hoping for help hunting for a potentially fictitious treasure. And after the recent events in Somnambula that had almost led her to retire and hang up her adventuring hat for good, Daring Do was likely to be wary of taking on too many new treasure-hunting jobs. She loved to work alone. But maybe, for Rainbow Dash, Daring Do might do a favor.

"Captain!" First Mate Mullet appeared at Celaeno's side. He held his claw to his forehead in salute. "Ship's in tip-top shape. She's ready for departure!"

"Thanks, Mullet." Celaeno nodded. "Great work! Now, get the rest of the scalawags to their stations and let's get her back in the open skies where she belongs."

"Aye aye!" Mullet shouted, and began delegating orders to the rest of the crew. Suddenly, Rainbow Dash felt the floorboards rumbling. The ship was finally leaving port! Or leaving her parents' house, rather.

Windy Whistles and Bow Hothoof stood on their porch, waving to the pirates and their daughter. "Have fun on your adventure!" Bow called out. "Be safe!"

"Don't forget to wear a sweater if it gets chilly out there!" Windy reminded them. "And if there's a gift shop, bring me back a plate!"

"We will!" shouted Mullet and Boyle in unison as they waved from the bow of the ship. "Thank ye for everything!" They'd grown quite fond of Rainbow Dash's parents and all their pampering. They sure were going to miss those delicious sandwiches.

Rainbow Dash trotted up to the edge of the ship and waved her hoof at her mom and dad. "Bye! See ya soon!"

Squabble jumped up and jangled the rope hooked to a giant brass bell. *DING-DONG!* It was the signal. "Up, up, and away!" whooped Captain Celaeno, and the brilliantly colored feathered wings of the airship spread open, carrying the ship off into the blue unknown.

CHAPTER SEVEN

Even though Daring Do lived on the far reaches of Equestria, it hadn't taken long to travel from Cloudsdale because Rainbow Dash knew the way by heart. She'd been to visit her adventuring friend on more than one occasion. The airship swooped low over the familiar forest of treetops and bore left. A gust of fresh, piney air rushed through Rainbow Dash's mane. "Over there!" she called out to

Celaeno, pointing to a clearing with a small cottage. The captain nodded in acknowledgment and steered to find a good place to land.

Once they were finally on the ground, the pirates prepared to disembark. In the process, Mullet and Boyle got into a spat about who should get to carry the treasure map. The two of them were best friends but often found silly ways to be competitive with each other.

Boyle grunted. "It's my turn to hold the treasure map. Just 'cause yer the first mate—"

"You'll rip it with yer hook!" Mullet sneered. "Give it back."

"Avast, me harpies!" Celaeno barked, snatching the map from their claws. "Rainbow Dash and I are going down there alone. Aye?"

"Aye *ayeeeee*," they parroted in defeat, and slumped off to go help Lix prepare dinner.

Tonight's menu was going to be stew, thanks to Windy and Bow's generous supply of potatoes. Somebird had to get peeling.

Rainbow Dash led the way through the trees and into Daring Do's clearing. "We should probably be extra polite, just to be safe," Rainbow Dash warned.

Captain Celaeno scrunched up her beak. "Why?"

"It's a long story." Rainbow Dash could feel the nerves bubbling up. Was this a huge mistake? Daring Do was so private. Rainbow Dash didn't want to keep barging in on her at every opportunity, but she did really need her advice and expertise this one time.

The rainbow-maned pony hesitantly knocked on the door. It immediately swung open, causing both Rainbow Dash and Captain Celaeno to jump in surprise. Daring Do was decked out in her adventure gear. "Rainbow Dash!" Daring Do smiled. "How nice to see ya."

"It is?" Rainbow Dash replied, completely relieved. "Okay, good. 'Cause I wasn't sure if—"

"And you are?" Daring Do interrupted as she sized up the captain and raised a suspicious brow. Her eyes darted to the captain's emerald peg leg and unusually large stature.

"Captain Celaeno of Ornithia and the Open Skies." She took off her big brown pirate's hat and bent into a deep bow. "At your service."

"Ah, I see. Please, come in! But don't touch anything." Daring Do motioned for them to enter. Captain Celaeno wasted no time, rushing inside. She thought she was being sneaky, but Rainbow Dash could tell that she was already reading all the plaques on the walls and the spines of the books.

"Rainbow Dash?" Daring Do whispered once Celaeno was out of earshot. "Why'd you bring one of the most untrustworthy rapscallions in all the kingdoms—*a pirate*—to my house?"

✦ ✦ ✦ ✦ ✦

After Rainbow Dash had explained the situation—that the captain and her crew were her friends, not foes—Daring Do began to warm up to the idea of helping them. But she still seemed hesitant. She stared down at the scratchy map, which had been rolled out on her large wooden farm table and was being held down by tiny golden paperweights carved into the shapes of sphinxes.

"I've gone on treasure hunts near those regions before, and I must warn you...it will be dangerous." Daring Do's face remained serious. "Are you sure you want to search for this alleged Good Fortune Garnet even though you aren't sure it exists?"

"I know it does! It has to." Captain Celaeno stood up. "The whole reason my crew and I got stuck working for the Storm King was because of a similar relic that we came across—the Misfortune Malachite. It brings bad luck to whoever possesses it!" Captain Celaeno watched as Daring Do's face changed. "The garnet has to be its opposite, right?"

"Is that a thing?" Rainbow Dash wondered aloud and took a sip from the goblet of apple cider Daring Do had offered to them as refreshment.

"I can't believe I'm saying this but…yes. The captain's logic is sound." Daring Do nodded, thinking back to all the relics she'd encountered in her long career. "Oftentimes, a magical relic has a polar opposite, with opposite properties. Just look at the Doomed Diadem of Xilati and the Tiara of Teotlale…"

"So the Good Fortune Garnet is *real*?!" Rainbow Dash spat out her cider. This was some big news. She wondered what other stuff she'd heard about at school and written off as just a bedtime story. "Then we *have* to find it! And I have to bring it back to Cloudsdale where it belongs!" Rainbow Dash's eyes met Celaeno's, and for a brief moment, they seemed to have a strange look to them. But it passed in a flash and Rainbow Dash found herself wondering if she'd imagined it.

"That's what I've been trying to tell you, Dash," Captain Celaeno smirked and gave her signature wink. "You'll be a hero yet."

Daring Do shot Rainbow Dash a funny look, then turned back to the parrot. "Why are you so invested in Rainbow Dash becoming a hero, Celaeno?"

"Because she and her friends were the ones who helped my crew members break free from the shackles of the Storm King. If they hadn't shown up and reminded us who we were, we might still all be lugging bags of sand and Storm King merchandise across the skies!"

The answer seemed to satisfy Daring Do well enough, which made Rainbow Dash glad. She knew that her old pal was suspicious of anycreature and everycreature, but this interrogation felt as if it was dragging on forever. And now that Rainbow Dash had some sort of tangible evidence that the Good Fortune Garnet was out there, just waiting to be rescued by *her*, she couldn't wait. They had to get this airship going immediately!

"So, Daring Do..." Rainbow Dash stood up. She lowered her head and raised her eyebrows. It was her best "convincing somepony" face. "Are you with us? Do you have any information that can help us on our journey?"

"Well, I did have plans to go research the Crystal Sphere of Khumn, but I do know something—or rather, some*pony* who can help you find the Garnet...." Daring Do admitted.

"All right!" Rainbow Dash shouted as Captain Celaeno let out a whoop. "So that means yes?"

"I'll help you on one condition." Daring Do

looked directly at Captain Celaeno. "That if we do succeed in locating it, the Good Fortune Garnet goes directly back to Cloudsdale."

"*Pshhht!*" Rainbow Dash laughed and rolled her eyes. "Where else would it go?"

"Nowhere I can think of!" Celaeno chirped, her voice audibly higher than usual. "Now, are we ready or are we going to sit around chit-chatting about it all day? Come on!"

And with that, the two ponies and the parrot captain were off to the ship to enjoy a dinner of pirate potato stew and a thrilling adventure searching for a priceless relic long lost.

CHAPTER EIGHT

The ragtag band of pirates and ponies had been flying in the airship for nearly three days before they caught their first glimpse of their destination. Alto Terre was a secluded village perched high up in the Unicorn Mountain Range, and Daring Do seemed to believe that it would help lead them to the location of the Good Fortune Garnet. Over the course of the journey, Daring Do had plenty of time to regale the pirates with many tales of her travels across Equestria and beyond. So she spared no details when describing her last journey to the region and all its odd quirks.

Naturally, the pirates had lots of questions about Alto Terre, but Rainbow Dash seemed to know the answers to almost all of them already. She explained that it was from reading a book called *Daring Do and the Forbidden City of Clouds*. Rainbow Dash explained everything from the Unicorn ponies' dislike of visitors to their odd, monochromatic manes and hides. Daring Do nodded along, looking somewhat proud. When Rainbow Dash finally finished talking, Daring Do gathered everycreature and briefed them on their mission.

"So when we get there, Rainbow Dash and I will go talk to Brumby first. He won't be forthcoming with his information about the Good Fortune Garnet if he feels that too many strangers are around. He'll feel like we're ambushing him." Then Daring Do shook her head and warned, "And trust me—once Brumby's good opinion is lost, it's gone for good." The pirates just shrugged and nodded. That was a concept they understood pretty well. Pirates didn't take guff from anycreature.

"Wait a second! We're going to meet Brumby Cloverpatch?!" Rainbow Dash squealed with unfettered excitement. "Like, the *actual* Earth pony adventurer? That is seriously cool."

"Should we recognize that name?" Captain Celaeno and the others were surprised by

Rainbow Dash's reaction. Was this some sort of pony celebrity? There was still so much to learn about Equestria.

"He's the aeronaut explorer pony from the books," Rainbow Dash explained, pacing back and forth. Her hooves clopped against the wooden deck as she talked, almost as if they were the punctuation to her words. "He has this really neat airship kinda like you guys, except his is called the *Reflector* 'cause it's all silver and shiny and when it's in the clouds it looks practically invisible—"

"Airship?" Mullet asked, a nervous expression on his face. "Do...uh...a lot of ponies have airships?"

"He's the only one I've ever heard of. I mean, Twilight has her hot-air balloon, but that's not really the same thing...." Rainbow Dash frowned, growing suspicious. Boyle and Mullet were acting quite squirmy. "Why?"

Boyle made a face and nudged Mullet so he'd stop asking so many questions. That guy was always getting them into trouble by flapping his big ol' beak. "No reason!" Boyle barked as the pair disappeared down the stairs to the quarters belowdecks. Rainbow Dash quickly brushed it off and turned back to the matter at hoof—Alto Terre.

Her heart quickened as the ship began to slow, descending toward a clear ridge scooped out of the side of the mountain, just a short staircase away from the village. Rainbow Dash scanned the horizon for signs of Brumby Cloverpatch. She was pretty sure she would recognize him instantly.

"All claws on deck, moving portside!"

ordered Captain Celaeno, and the crew scrambled to their positions. The parrots heaved and hoed, pulling the wingspan in with their brute strength until finally the ship was positioned. Once they'd safely made anchor, Captain Celaeno tipped her hat to Rainbow Dash and Daring Do. "We'll be here waiting for you."

The two Pegasi took off, flying up over the stairs with Daring Do leading the way. Rainbow Dash had been instructed not to talk to anypony until they got to Brumby's cottage, so she zipped her muzzle and kept close behind.

"Hey, who are you?" a mint-colored Unicorn stallion wearing an emerald-green sash called out as they trotted through the main gates of the village. "And what do you want? State your business in Alto Terre!" He'd positioned himself as a makeshift guard and this was the first instance in which his job had ever mattered.

"Just visiting a friend." Daring Do smiled and waved her hoof nonchalantly. "Have a nice day." Rainbow Dash followed suit, flashing him a friendly smile. He looked confused, but for lack of a better plan just decided to accept it. Nopony else said anything to the duo, but ponies were definitely staring. Rainbow Dash was starting to understand why Daring Do had been so insistent that Captain Celaeno and the rest of the birds stay behind. If these ponies were reacting strangely to some Pegasi, who knew what they'd do if they saw a bunch of gigantic parrots with peg legs, hooks, and eye patches?

They turned off the main cobblestoned road and into a little alleyway, away from the hoof traffic of the shops and taverns. Standing at the end of the alleyway was a curious little cottage that was distinctly different from the rest of the buildings. It looked like something Discord would have chosen—a patchwork quilt of colors with its blue shutters, red door, and wavy stripes of teal painted across the facade. The thatched roof reminded Rainbow Dash of the houses back in Ponyville, and the curious selection of dainty clouds circling above it like a halo elicited memories of the dwellings in Cloudsdale.

"Brace yourself." Daring Do muttered the warning under her breath. "He might not be too happy to see you."

CHAPTER NINE

Daring Do lifted her hoof and held it in mid-air for a moment, as if she were reconsidering what she was about to do. But they had come too far not to find out if Brumby could help. She knocked softly on the red wooden door. It swung open to reveal a scruffy stallion with a top hat squashed down on his graying mane.

Daring Do smirked at the sight of him. He looked like a mess. "Brumby, old pal."

"Daring Do?" Brumby's eyes lit up with recognition of his friend. "What a surprise!" The last time he'd seen her was during a visit to the southern bit of Equestria to meet with the Aeronauts Society. They'd caught up over lunch and she'd told him all about how she'd written a book based on their adventure in Cirrostrata. But that was at least a few years back.

"Come in! Come in!" He waved his hoof and waddled inside. He looked back over his shoulder at Rainbow Dash, unable to hide his annoyance. "Who's that?"

"This is my friend Rainbow Dash," Daring Do explained. Rainbow Dash gave a tiny nod and a smile but didn't say a peep. Daring Do sat down on a purple stool and gestured to Rainbow Dash, who did the same. "Don't worry—I trust her completely."

"All right, if ya say so." Brumby trotted to the kitchen and returned with two glasses of Alto Terran pear juice. He passed one to Daring Do and looked as if he was going to keep the other for himself, but then gave it to Rainbow Dash. "So what do ya want to know 'bout this time?"

Daring Do reached into her shirt for Rainbow Dash's sloppily drawn fillyhood map and unrolled it on the table. "Does this place ring any bells?"

"The Thunder Jungle?" Brumby traced it with his hoof, narrowing his eyes. A sense of darkness shrouded his face. "Why do ya want to go there?"

"Well, supposedly there's this ancient Pegasus treasure called the Good—"

"Fortune Garnet," Brumby finished. "The

gem that makes great things happen to ya, right?" Rainbow Dash and Daring Do perked up and looked at each other. So he did know about the treasure they were looking for! The pirates were going to be so excited when the ponies returned with actual information beyond a filly's map. Rainbow Dash had been able tell that Celaeno had been doubting this little pit stop, but it was all turning out to be worth it.

"So it's real?" Daring Do marveled. Up until this moment, Daring Do hadn't realized her doubts about finding such a relic were so strong.

"If it still exists, then sure it is." Brumby stood up and hobbled over to a basket brimming with yellowed scrolls. They were rolled up tight with blue ribbon. He pawed through the collection and selected one. "Back in the early days of traveling around in the *Reflector*, I dabbled in cartography. It only made sense since I was watching the landscape from above for hours everyday. Gets to be a bit a tedious after a while, ya know?"

It felt as if he was speaking directly to Rainbow Dash, so she nodded to show she was interested in his story. "Totally!"

"When I came across that swirling mass of a storm, of course I tracked it on my map." Brumby rolled out his own scroll on top of Rainbow Dash's scribbly version from school, and it was as if the map had come to life. There were hills and valleys, silvery streams snaking through the fields, and tiny villages dotted throughout. In the bottom left corner of the map was the blustery black cloud. Just like in Rainbow Dash's version. "Of course I had to land my ship at the nearest village and ask 'em about the unusual weather."

Rainbow Dash was now perched on the edge of her stool. If she leaned any farther, she would have toppled to the floor. "What did they say?!"

"That it had been that way for hundreds o' years, all on account of some Pegasus who had a powerful Unicorn cast a weather spell on the jungle, so he could hide and protect his precious garnet there. Legend has it that the thunderclouds are impenetrable."

Rainbow Dash was confused. "If nopony could get through it, then how would he get to his precious relic?"

"There's some special Pegasus weather trick that only a few of ya can do, I guess?" Brumby shrugged and reached for the map.

"A trick?" Daring Do racked her brain. Most Pegasi could perform simple weather maneuvers, but she wasn't sure what move would allow one to bust through an impassable wall. "That doesn't make any sense."

"Beats me. I'd never go near that Thunder Jungle, anyhow." He began to roll up the map, but Daring Do interrupted him.

"Do you mind if we borrow that?" she asked slyly.

"I suppose there's no harm in it," the old stallion replied. He tied the blue ribbon back around the scroll and tossed it to Daring Do. "But just know you're chasin' an impossible prize!"

"I think we can manage." Daring Do laughed as she turned to Rainbow Dash. She held out the map, gave her comrade a little wink, and whispered, "You take this back to the ship and go ahead. I'm sure the captain is getting anxious."

"You're not coming?" Rainbow Dash replied, crestfallen.

"I am," Daring Do insisted. "But I can't just show up and leave already." She gestured to Brumby. He looked as if he was trying to eavesdrop, and he wasn't really very good at hiding it. "I should visit with my old friend for a bit. I'll fly to meet the ship in the skies!" At this, Brumby smiled and Rainbow Dash understood. If Fluttershy or Applejack had shown up to visit after not seeing her for years, she would demand that they stay until they were all caught up.

"Okay! See ya later!" Rainbow Dash called out and took off to find the pirates at port. Ten minutes later, Daring Do and Brumby spotted the magnificent airship take off and disappear into the clouds. When the colored feathers of the ship's sail extended out, Daring Do's friend had an odd reaction.

"*That* was the ship you were talking about?!" Brumby cried out in despair. He stomped his hoof on the ground and gritted his teeth. "This is an outrage!"

"I don't understand—"

"Those are the pirates who *robbed* me on the *Reflector*! Did I just give ya *my* map to help them?"

"I...uh...I..." Daring Do was at a loss for words and, apparently, her own good sense.

CHAPTER TEN

Daring Do! I can't believe *you*, of all ponies, are in cahoots with those sky scoundrels!" Brumby Cloverpatch growled with disdain. "They're the worst kind of adventurers—only looking out for their own interests!" He grabbed a saddlebag and began to throw items into it, barely paying attention to anything he selected. Daring Do watched as he tossed in a bag of marbles, a block of cheddar cheese, five apples, and a rubber duck. "Please tell me that ya sensed it, too? Somethin' off about 'em?"

"Well, I…" Daring Do hesitated. She'd be lying if she said she hadn't gotten a strange feeling when Rainbow Dash had led the pirates to her door. The way Captain Celaeno had been so interested in the Good Fortune Garnet and then was noticeably quiet when Rainbow Dash had proclaimed she would return it to Cloudsdale was suspicious. But Rainbow Dash believed them. "I *want* to trust them…?"

Brumby sighed, clearly exhausted by the fact that his friend could not see his point. "But ya can't."

"I don't think I understand," Daring Do said. She'd never run into sky pirates before Captain Celaeno and the crew had showed up on her own doorstep. How did Brumby have so many negative feelings about them? "Care to enlighten me?"

"I'll show ya." Brumby grunted and opened a drawer on his ancient Alto Terran wooden hutch. He yanked out a weathered sketchbook. It was fat with loose drawings and looked as if it was one piece of paper away from bursting. Daring Do flipped it open and immediately understood. They were diagrams! Intricate plans for all sorts of inventions.

But there was one drawing that kept popping up on every page. It was a design for a prototype backpack that would allow landlocked ponies to fly. Daring Do immediately recalled seeing the exact devices belowdecks on Celaeno's airship! The parrots had even given her a demonstration of the way they worked with Mullet and Boyle buzzing around the ship like two enormous, feathered flies. "They told me they bartered for those sky-packs!"

"Bartered?" Brumby took off his hat and smoothed his graying mane. He looked angry. He shook his hoof in the air. "*Stole* is more like it! They offered to help with the final tweaks and test them in exchange for a few for themselves, but I haven't seen them since." He'd been working on that invention for years and finally managed to build enough to bring to the Aeronauts Society Convention this year. He was going to blow them all away.

"I knew something was fishy about those birds." Daring Do shook her head. "Captain Celaeno insisted that she just wanted to help Rainbow Dash find the garnet. I should have trusted my instincts. Should I go back to their ship and retrieve the sky-packs for you?"

"No, I've got a much better idea." Brumby held up the saddlebag, now bulging with ridiculous items. His eyes were wild with excitement. It was as if he'd finally awoken from a long nap. "We're going to steal something that *they* want. Show 'em how it feels!"

Daring Do cocked her head to the side. "Do you mean . . . the Good Fortune Garnet?"

"My dear, that's exactly what I'm suggestin'." Brumby nodded. "We're gonna get to it first." He didn't even let Daring Do weigh in on his plan before he galloped out of the cottage, heading for the hills where he kept his own ship.

As she ran through the narrow streets of Alto Terre to the *Reflector*'s docking bay, Daring Do's mind drifted to Rainbow Dash, alone on the ship with those pirates and waiting for her to join them. If anypony could handle herself on a ship full of deceitful scalawags, it would be her. Hopefully Rainbow Dash would understand that Daring Do had to look out for the old aeronaut on his wild mission.

It was now officially a race to the relic. And there was no way Brumby was letting the wrong claws get ahold of it without a fight. Daring Do, however, still couldn't work out which side she was on.

CHAPTER ELEVEN

The captain's quarters were spacious enough, kitted out with a large wooden table, two luxurious velvet sofas, and a stained oak desk where the captain could conduct her important pirate business affairs. But even with all of its comforts, Rainbow Dash was beginning to feel cramped. Captain Celaeno, Mullet, and Rainbow Dash had been cooped up inside for hours, charting a course into the Thunder Jungle that might inflict the least amount of damage to the ship.

"If we come at it from above, maybe we can lower the ship down fast—like a load of cargo onto a dock?" Mullet suggested. "Rainbow Dash, what do ye think?"

"Yeah, that could work...." Rainbow Dash replied, not even knowing what the question had been. It was difficult for Rainbow Dash to pay attention when she still had no clue what had become of Daring Do after her encounter with Brumby Cloverpatch. Daring Do had told her she'd be right behind them, and flying to catch up should have been a breeze for her. Unless her bad wing was acting up again? Maybe that was it. Or perhaps once she'd gotten to visiting with her old pal Brumby, the two of them lost track of time. Rainbow Dash tried to tell herself that it was a tangible reason, but something in the pit of her stomach was telling her otherwise.

Rainbow Dash didn't think the Good Fortune Garnet was worth putting a friend in danger. But Daring Do wasn't any normal friend. She'd faced even more dangers than Rainbow Dash. Daring Do would be just fine…right? Rainbow Dash looked at Brumby's intricate map on the table and marveled at the various details that had been left out of the version she'd drawn in school.

"You all right, Rainbow Dash?" Celaeno asked with genuine concern in her voice. "You seem down. Was it because of dinner? I'm really sorry about that.…" It had been Squabble's turn to prepare the meal since Lix Spittle had the day off. Instead of making a hearty potato stew like usual, he'd decided to get creative and make his special "birdseed casserole." It was basically gruel with burnt birdseed crusted on top. Rainbow Dash had only managed one bite before giving up and sharing her last pasta-and-potato sandwich with the others when Squabble wasn't looking. But that wasn't what was bothering her.

She had much bigger concerns on her mind. Rainbow Dash had to find out what had happened to her friend.

"Oh no," Rainbow Dash insisted. "I'm fine, really. I'm just feeling a bit cramped. Maybe I just need a wing stretch?" She yawned, stood up, and trotted to the door. "I'm gonna go fly alongside the ship for a while."

Captain Celaeno acknowledged her with a nod and turned her attention back to the map on the table. Rainbow Dash could hear her cursing the fact that there was no *X* to mark the spot. After they'd found the Thunder Jungle and landed, how were they to locate the garnet? It would basically be like flying blind.

Outside, the sky had turned from a pretty, cloudless blue to an ominous gray. No creature seemed to notice. Most of the pirate crew was napping belowdecks. While they slept, the fog was growing thick enough that the grassy fields below were almost undetectable. Rainbow Dash burst through a dense patch and kicked it away, obliterating it with her weather-pony skills. But within a matter of seconds, it rolled back into place. She'd never seen fog perform so strangely.

Rainbow Dash quickly developed a system of kicking through the weird fog and poking her head into the cleared view for a quick look, hoping to see Daring Do flying up to join them. But her adventuring friend was still nowhere to be found.

After an hour of kicking and peeking, the Pegasus's wings began to slow with fatigue. Rainbow Dash decided to muster her energy and give one last kick before giving up. If she didn't see anything, she'd just go back to her hammock in the crew's quarters and fall asleep.

"Come on!" Rainbow Dash yelled, flying at top speed and kicking her hooves out with every ounce of strength in her body. The fog blasted away, creating the largest circular window yet. The edges swirled and pulsed, keeping the fog at bay just barely long enough for

Rainbow Dash to take in the landscape ahead. The sight of it shook her to the core.

"*Uhh...* mateys?!" Rainbow Dash called out to the pirates. "I think you're gonna want to come above deck to see this!" The airship was headed straight for a dark, blustery mass the size of Canterlot. It hardly looked like the drawing on Brumby's map.

"I knew it was real!" Captain Celaeno appeared at the helm, wind rushing through her feathers. She was invigorated by the impending challenge. "That means we're close to the Good Fortune Garnet," she breathed in awe. "It's in there somewhere, and soon it will be ours. I mean—*Cloudsdale's.*"

Rainbow Dash landed back on deck next to Celaeno. "It looks pretty intense.... Are we

sure we want to take the ship through that?"
As soon as the words left Rainbow Dash's lips,
the airship shot forward like a catapult. The
storm was sucking them in!

There was no turning back now.

CHAPTER TWELVE

It had been a few weeks since Brumby had taken the *Reflector* out for a spin, and he'd missed it. The ship had always been a reliable old gal. The Earth pony aeronaut had traveled hundreds of miles in it—everywhere from the far reaches of Southern Equestria up to the Frozen North. He loved exploring Equestria and surveying the land below for his detailed maps. Nothing was better than the fresh air and a gentle ride.

Today, however, the airship sputtered along in erratic movements. Instead of the smooth sailing he was used to, sudden surges of power caused the *Reflector* to arc up into the sky, only to dramatically drop back down again. The aeronaut couldn't seem to get the ride to level out no matter how much he tweaked the controls.

Brumby peered over the edge of the railing. The sprawling green landscape below appeared much closer than he was comfortable with. "We're losing altitude!" he called out to Daring Do, then craned his neck back to inspect the silvery balloon's heating mechanisms one more time. Everything *looked* normal. Brumby sighed with frustration. "I just don't know what's trippin' her up, Do!"

"Maybe the malfunction is on the topside?" Daring Do suggested. She spread her wings. "I'm going to fly up there and check it out."

The shimmering mirror effect of the *Reflector*'s balloon allowed the ship to appear nearly invisible in the skies, so it was difficult to detect at first, but there was a massive tear in the fabric. Air was leaking out at a rapid pace. No wonder they'd been having trouble. "We've got a puncture," she called down to Brumby. "I might be able to repair it on my own, but you'll have to guide me through it."

Brumby dug through his emergency patch kit, grumbling to himself. "This wouldn't be a problem if those scalawags hadn't robbed me of my sky-packs! I could just strap one on my back, zoom up there, and fix it myself—"

Out of nowhere, a black squall blasted the ship, causing it to sway and fall several feet.

But this time, the *Reflector* didn't soar back up again. "She's falling!" The wind began to pick up, making things even worse. Brumby cried out in horror, hooking his hooves through the safety straps on the side of railing. "We're going down, Daring Do!"

"Not if I have anything to say about it, we're not!"

As the ship began to plummet, Daring Do had to think fast. She flew down below the balloon, wings beating at full force against the gathering gusts of wind. Daring Do dug deep, using every ounce of strength she had to support the airship as it tumbled down, picking up speed in its descent to the ground. The pony braced herself against the bottom of the hull, hooves and wings outspread.

She just hoped there was something soft below.

CHAPTER THIRTEEN

The blackened clouds were thick and swirling. Brilliant bolts of lightning shot through the sky in intricate designs, followed by deafening claps of thunder. It was like a giant force field of weather patterns in the shape of a dome.

Rainbow Dash was starting to doubt that a secret jungle could even exist somewhere deep inside the dark mass. Maybe this whole story of the Good Fortune Garnet was just another tall tale, after all. However, Brumby's words about the Good Fortune Garnet and the storm surrounding it kept echoing in Rainbow Dash's head. He'd called it "impenetrable." That meant no pony, or bird, could get inside no matter how hard they tried. But somehow, the storm was still pulling the ship closer. They needed a plan to either get in...or get out. Far out.

"I wonder why they call it the 'Thunder Jungle'?" Captain Celaeno joked in a feeble attempt to make light of the scary scene in front of them. In reality, she had absolutely no idea how they were going to penetrate the dark cloud wall. All she knew was that she had to.

"What're we gonna do, Cap'n?" Boyle scratched his head feathers. He'd only seen a storm like this once before, when that monster who'd called himself the Storm King had had tried to take over Equestria. "The ship can't make it through those clouds and 'bolts."

"Mullet?" Celaeno frowned. She often looked to her first mate for his opinion. "What do you think?"

"I'm 'fraid Boyle's right," Mullet agreed. "We'd be fried by lightning before we even made it past the first layer."

Boyle clicked his beak. "I'm not sure this treasure is worth the gamble...." The crew broke out in a cacophony of squawks. Everybird was chattering and plotting about how to turn the ship back. There was plenty of treasure to be had elsewhere in the skies. Why did they need this one jewel so very badly?

"Scalawags!" Captain Celaeno hollered, causing the crew to fall silent. She put her claws behind her back and began pacing the deck. "Who are we?"

"Swashbuckling treasure hunters," the crew said in unison, except for Squabble, who just squawked.

Celaeno grinned with pride. She loved the sound of that. She leaped across the deck and posed, triumphant, propping her peg leg on a box and her claws on her hips. "And what do we do?!"

Lix Spittle scratched her head with a wooden spoon. "*Uhhh . . . we swash?*"

"Buckle!" yelled Boyle, pumping his hook-claw into the air.

"And hunt treasure!" the rest of them hollered together.

"That's right." Like every captain, Celaeno loved to deliver a good inspirational speech to her crew now and then, even if they didn't want to hear it. She was just getting started. "We've traveled far and wide across these skies—both as masters of our own fate and as facilitators of someone else's. Tell me, mateys...which one was better?"

The pirates looked to one another and shrugged.

"Masters of your own fate!" Rainbow Dash answered with the gusto that the captain was looking for.

"That's right!" Celaeno laughed. She began to pace down the line, looking each pirate in the eyes, except for Squabble. His eyes lolled around in different directions. "We *chose* this here journey to challenge ourselves. It didn't choose us!" Celaeno looked right at Rainbow Dash. "Besides, after the Storm

King's rule, didn't we all decide to be awesome again?"

There was a loud collective grumble of confirmation.

"That's what I thought!" Celaeno cheered in satisfaction. "Now, Rainbow Dash..."

"Yeah, Captain?" Rainbow Dash replied, unable to tear her gaze away from the frightening storm. They were almost there.

"Pegasi can manipulate the weather, right?" There was scheming look in Celaeno's black-lined eyes, but her voice had a nervous quality to it. She was scared! Her whole speech had been to pump up herself, too.

"Usually, but *that* thing"—Rainbow Dash pointed to the dark mass—"is totally uncharted territory!"

"Maybe a little Rainbow magic might help?" Captain Celaeno suggested. "You dad mentioned at the Weather Factory tour that the Sonic Rainboom is the most powerful trick a Pegasus can do...."

"Whoa!" Rainbow Dash lit up. "You're right! I don't know why I didn't think of it before...." All she had to do was fly as fast as she could, right into the storm. And since they were barreling straight toward it, Rainbow Dash didn't waste another second. "See you inside the jungle, mateys!" she shouted before taking a running leap off the ship.

Rainbow Dash soared through the foggy air at top speed, leaving the vessel in her wake. She focused on the flashes of lightning, pushing herself to reach the wall before one of them could touch the ship. Suddenly, a beautiful blast of rainbow colors exploded in a giant ring of light! The resulting rift allowed the airship to sail right through, untouched by the raging storm.

CHAPTER FOURTEEN

Brumby untied his hoof from the strap and climbed out of the ship, thanking his lucky stars that Daring Do had been with him to discover the hole in his balloon. What would he have done without her? The *Reflector* would have been smashed to bits in this unfamiliar landscape.

"Well, that just put us behind the pirates!" The old stallion squinted, unable to place the scenery in his mind's map. "Where are we?" There were some colorful shapes in the distance. They were too blurry to make out, but they looked to be approaching their crash site. "And what are those things? I thought this area was Changeling territory."

Brumby wasn't entirely sure whether he hadn't hit his head on something in the commotion of it all. "They're so...bright and colorful?" Normally, the region would be barren and devoid of any vegetation. But this spot was lush with foliage.

"It's just a bunch of exotic flowers," Daring Do said without even looking up. "But there's nothing to worry about—we should be far out of the regions for Somnambular Blooms and Poison Joke. So, smell away!" She trotted around the side of the balloon to better assess the damage. Luckily, Daring had helped slow the bulk of the weight on the descent. There were just a few small spots to repair, along with a patch-up job on the balloon. It wouldn't take too long, and hopefully it wasn't enough of a setback to put them of out the running.

"No, not the flowers." Brumby stomped his hoof for emphasis. "Those!"

A swarm of pony-like creatures with bug wings and strange solid-color eyes were flying right toward them. They were varying shades of green, yellow, and purple, and appeared to have beetle shells on their backs. Daring Do finally tore her eyes away from the task of patching the balloon to look up. "Oh, those are just Changelings."

"Aren't Changelings all black and blue, with lil' holes in their hooves, though?"

"They used to be." Daring Do shrugged as if the news she was delivering wasn't totally mind-blowing. "But they changed."

"Well, shouldn't we hide or somethin'?" Brumby dug into his saddlebag to find anything that might help them defend themselves, but all he managed to pull out was his rubber duck. "Changelings are evil! They suck the love right out of ya."

"Actually, now we just spread love and friendship!" a chipper voice chimed in. The entire swarm was standing right next to the balloon. The tallest of the bunch was lime green with spiky orange horns and glittering purple wings. He smiled and gave a small bow. "Hello! I'm Thorax, and I'm the leader of the Changelings. What are your names?"

"Uh...er..."

It seemed Brumby was speechless, so Daring Do wiped off her hooves and trotted over. She tipped her pith helmet at Thorax. "The name's Do. Daring Do. Pleasure to meet ya."

"Did you need some assistance?" Thorax gestured to the broken vehicle. He stared at Brumby, who just blinked in disbelief. Thorax always forgot that ponies still remembered Changelings as monsters, so the reaction was a little jarring. He was just trying to help.

"With what?" Daring Do was already back to the task at hoof: working on fixing the ship. If they wanted a chance at recovering the Good Fortune Garnet before Captain Celaeno got her claws on it, they couldn't waste any time.

"Your vessel." Thorax pointed to a damaged section. The wood plank was jutting out of the side in a sad way. "We can fix it for you!"

"Changelings know how to fix airships?" Brumby finally asked. Apparently everything he'd previously thought about the creatures was entirely wrong.

"We can do a lot of things." Thorax laughed. "Now that we have time to focus on learning and having fun with our friends instead of feasting on the love of others, we've discovered that we're quite quick at picking up new skills! May we try?"

Brumby was about to protest, but the sight of his dear ship in such disrepair tugged at his heartstrings. If these Changelings could fix her, then it was worth a shot. "Okay, have at it."

Daring Do and Brumby stood back as Thorax gave the signal. The Changelings surrounded the airship, flitting their buggy wings and humming as they worked. Less than a minute later, they stood back. The *Reflector* was as good as new!

"I don't believe it...." Brumby muttered. He trotted around the ship three times with his mouth agape. "That's incredible!" The Changelings bowed, faces beaming with pride. "I don't know how to thank ya enough."

"We owe you one," Daring Do agreed with a nod.

"It was our pleasure." Thorax grinned. "But if you truly wish to thank us, you can spread word on your travels—Changelings do have the power to change! We have discovered the Magic of Friendship and can't wait to make more friends throughout Equestria."

"We will," Daring Do assured them. She

reached her hoof out to help Brumby back up the steps and onto the airship. "Sorry to leave so quickly, but we're in a . . . race."

"Oh, then you have to go right away! Safe travels!" Thorax again bent into a deep bow and the others followed suit. "Come back and visit the Changeling kingdom anytime, new friends!" The bug creatures waved their hooves as the airship began to float up into the sky.

Thanks to the unexpected help from the Changelings, the *Reflector* was back in action and working even better than it had before. Now all it had to do was survive the worst storm of all time.

CHAPTER FIFTEEN

Thanks to Brumby Cloverpatch, Rainbow Dash knew the story about the Good Fortune Garnet and where it had been hiding all these years. But the Thunder Jungle still was the most peculiar thing to witness. On the other side of the raging lightning storm was a stunning oasis filled with waterfalls and luscious plants. It was its own ecosystem, untouched by pony hooves.

"Why is it so dark in here?" Mullet asked,

traipsing down the gangplank and jumping onto the soft moss. "It was the middle of the afternoon before we came through the storm."

"That is pretty weird," Rainbow Dash agreed. She had noticed it, too. It was as dark as if it were the middle of the night, except there was a slight red glow over everything. It was as if the whole crew had time traveled or stepped into another dimension. Maybe they had.

"I think it's because of the thunder shield," Captain Celaeno theorized. "Sunlight can't get inside here because it's being blocked out by those storm clouds. Look at where we entered." She pointed her claw up to the spot where Rainbow Dash had performed her Sonic Rainboom and permeated the thick clouds. Light streamed in as a beam, but only from that one circle. It was like a Bridleway spotlight.

The rest of the pirates trudged off the ship and waited for their next orders. "So where's the treasure, Cap'n?" Boyle looked around at the darkness and pulled out a pair of night-vision goggles. "Let's find it and get out outta here. This place creeps me out!"

"What's with the red light?" Lix Spittle squawked. Squabble nodded in agreement. Then the two walked off together to go splash water from the stream onto their faces and share theories.

"Any ideas, Rainbow Dash?" Captain Celaeno looked around, desperate. Perhaps she was worried about looking bad in front of her fellow pirates. No captain wanted to lead his or her crew on an aimless treasure hunt and leave without a prize to show for it at the end! "Do you remember anything else from the stories? Any clue to where it might be?"

"*I* do," a familiar voice answered. But it was not Rainbow Dash. Standing in the nearby grove of palm trees and ferns was none other than Daring Do and Brumby Cloverpatch! Neither of them looked very happy.

"How did you—" Celaeno blinked her eyes in disbelief. She looked to the two ponies and then to the rift in the cloud dome. The *Reflector* must have entered the jungle right behind their ship, but it had appeared invisible to them because of its unique reflective properties.

"It's true! I remember lots of details 'bout this Good Fortune Garnet story," Brumby barked. "But I'm not sure I want to share that information"—he trotted closer, keeping his eye on

Captain Celaeno all the while—"with a bunch of thieves!" Brumby could tell from the shock on her face that he was one pony she wasn't expecting to see again so soon.

"Brumby!" Rainbow Dash called out. She put her hooves up, pleading. "We're all here for the same the reason, right?" Rainbow Dash gave a little smile. "We all want to find the garnet and bring it back to Cloudsdale and—"

"No," Daring Do interrupted, shaking her head. "Not all of us..."

"What do you mean?" Rainbow Dash was seriously confused. Brumby was staring at Celaeno. "Okay...did I miss something here?"

"That's not important!" Captain Celaeno insisted. "Whatever may have happened in the past is not relevant here right now. Rainbow Dash is right—we're all in this together. And

I don't know about the rest of you scalawags, but I'd like to spend the least amount of time in this place as possible...." Her face looked even more intense than usual in the eerie red light.

"She's right," Daring Do chimed in. "Let's find the garnet and we can settle this after. Brumby?"

The old stallion grunted in annoyance and then gave in. "Fine."

"So...you said you knew something that could help us?" Rainbow Dash reminded. She scratched the dirt with her hoof. "Did it happen to be where X marks the spot?"

"Not quite, but almost." Brumby smirked. He held his hoof up to demonstrate. It was shrouded in red light. "All ya have to do...is follow the glow."

The pirates were momentarily stumped.

Finally, Captain Celaeno put two and two together. "Of course! Garnets are red, right? The Good Fortune Garnet is the source of the red light! Once we find that…we're as good as golden."

CHAPTER SIXTEEN

The red glow was becoming stronger with each hoofstep into the forest. Rainbow Dash didn't like to admit it, but she was feeling a tiny bit spooked. She trotted close behind Captain Celaeno, who trudged forward with purpose through the labyrinth of tropical trees and foliage. Nothing seemed to faze her. "This way!" Celaeno shouted to the group before taking a sharp left, then a hard right. "No, maybe it's this way...."

This pattern seemed to go on for hours. Rainbow Dash felt like giving up. Her hooves were tired and her tummy was growling, despite being gifted a piece of cheese by Brumby a few miles back. She was about to suggest they abandon the whole mission when Captain Celaeno stopped dead in her tracks.

"I see it," she said in disbelief. "Look, everycreature! It's right there."

The pirates rushed forward, clamoring to get a look at the treasure. Squabble was caught behind Mullet and Boyle, so he tried climbing onto their backs. But his attempt was unsuccessful and he came tumbling to the ground. Brumby, Rainbow Dash, and Daring Do were finally able to push their way through the bumbling pirates to catch a glimpse.

The jagged, glowing red stone was simply

sitting in the middle of a stone slab. There was no elaborate protection system around it or carvings depicting its history. It was as if somepony had just dropped it there a few hours ago and would be back for it at any moment. It was ripe for the taking.

Captain Celaeno couldn't help herself. She lunged forward, eyes glowing red with the reflection of the stone as she clasped her claws around it. But as soon as she tried to lift it up, the parrot realized that it was either stuck... or it was unbelievably heavy. "I can't seem to—" She grunted, squatting down and trying to leverage her own weight against it. Boyle and Mullet rushed over to help her, but they couldn't lift it, either. It was such a small rock—how could it weigh so much?

"Just as I thought!" Brumby's laugh cut

through the sounds of grunting as the pirates kept trying to extract the garnet in vain. "You did plan to keep the Good Fortune Garnet for yourself, Captain."

"What?" Captain Celaeno stood up, a look of feigned innocence on her face. How did this pony know her innermost thoughts? "I did not!"

"You're lying," Brumby explained. "Because if ya weren't, you'd be able to do this." He trotted over to the garnet and kicked it gently with his hoof. The gem rolled with ease, as if were weightless. "See, while we were trudging all over this jungle in circles, I remembered another thing about the garnet...."

By now the ponies and pirates were hanging on Brumby's every word. "The Good Fortune Garnet will only allow itself to be owned, to provide its gifts to a creature who wants to use it help others...not for personal gain."

"So that's why Celaeno can't pick it up?" Rainbow Dash was shocked. She felt as if the ground was falling out from under her hooves. "Because she wasn't going to give it back to Cloudsdale like she promised?" Rainbow Dash met Celaeno's eyes and instantly knew that Brumby was right. Her friend had been lying to her all along.

"Rainbow Dash!" Celaeno pleaded. "It wasn't like that...." The captain walked over to a large rock and sat down, letting out a heavy sigh.

Rainbow Dash raised an eyebrow. "So how was it, then?"

"I did originally want to help you and the ponies of Cloudsdale by returning the treasure to where it belonged, but the more I thought about it... the more I realized that my crew here has had more than their fair share of bad luck. First with the Misfortune Malachite, and then the Storm King... I guess I just wanted a way to make sure that all our future swash-buckling days would be great ones!"

"*Awww,* Cap'n," Mullet sniffed. "You were tryin' to take care of us. That's really sweet of you."

"Yeah," said Boyle, still tugging at the gem to no avail. "We just wanted the garnet to bring us riches."

"I'm really sorry, Rainbow Dash." Captain Celaeno took off her hat and slumped down. "And I'm sorry for not bringing your sky-packs back right away, Brumby. We meant to, but got caught up in our trip and just figured we'd get them to you on the way back. We'll return them to you as soon as possible."

Daring Do and Brumby exchanged a surprised look.

Celaeno stood up and hobbled over to the pirates. "Now, we should probably leave you to it, since we can't help with the garnet anyway. But if we could, we'd bring it back to Cloudsdale, where it belongs."

She tugged at Boyle's shirt to pull him away from his obsession with the gem, but lost her balance. The captain flailed her arms and tried to regain her footing, but it was no use. She stepped around the glowing gem, wobbly on her peg leg. The captain kicked the Good Fortune Garnet and it went spiraling into the air, headed straight for Rainbow Dash.

"Gotcha!" Rainbow Dash caught the gem

and nearly dropped it because of how light it actually was. A wide smile spread across her face as the realization hit her. "Captain Celaeno—you kicked the garnet! If you were able to move it, that means your intentions were true after all!" The pirate captain did really care about Rainbow Dash and the Pegasi of Cloudsdale.

"Huh." Brumby nodded, considering. "I guess Rainbow Dash is right. Maybe ya aren't such a bad old bird after all."

Captain Celaeno suddenly felt lighter than a cloud. "Shall we get this thing back to where it should be, then?" It was time for a new adventure.

"Sure, and after we bring Brumby back home, then we can return the Good Fortune Garnet, too!" Daring Do joked. Everycreature laughed, except Brumby, who grumbled something inaudible and began to trudge back to the airships.

As Rainbow Dash gave the gem to Daring Do for safekeeping, she felt a sense of calm wash over her. She'd tried her best and succeeded, and she'd done it with friends by her side. Her parents would be so proud.

CHAPTER SEVENTEEN

The crowd on the steps outside the Cloudsdale History Museum looked even larger than the one at the Wonderbolts' Loop-de-Loop Hoopla! There was a feeling of excitement in the air as Pegasi from all over the city arrived and waited patiently for the big reveal. They'd been hearing the myth about Cloudsdale's precious lost relic, the Good Fortune Garnet, their whole lives. Nopony ever expected it to be found, let alone by a few ponies and a band of bird pirates from beyond Equestria.

"It's almost time!" Rainbow Dash yelled to the group behind the curtain. They were all going to be onstage during the dedication. It was only right, since each of them had contributed to the precious gem's retrieval in some way.

There was Brumby Cloverpatch in his aeronaut's top hat and goggles standing beside a stoic Daring Do. Next to them were Windy Whistles and Bow Hothoof, decked out in their finest clothing and fighting back the tears of pride welling up in their eyes. And last but not least, Captain Celaeno and her ragtag pirate bird crew readied themselves, sporting their very own Brumby-designed pirate sky-packs.

Rainbow Dash could feel her heart bursting at the sheer awesomeness of the moment. All of them were there because they had achieved their goal together—as friends. "Is everycreature ready?"

"Aye aye!" Captain Celaeno cheered. "Let's show these little ponies what they've been missin'!"

Rainbow Dash took a deep breath and flew out to the platform, her friends and family following and positioning themselves behind her. "Citizens of Cloudsdale!" Rainbow Dash smiled. "We give you...the *Good Fortune Garnet!*" She grabbed the silken fabric that was covering the new display case and ripped it off in one dramatic motion. "This gem is dedicated to you!"

A collective reverent gasp hushed over the

Pegasi as they caught their first glimpse of the real, shimmering relic. It was not only beautiful, but everypony could feel the love from the shimmering stone. Ponies rushed the stage, crowding around for a better look. Rainbow Dash and her pals stepped out of the way, laughing.

"Hey, Captain?" Rainbow Dash nudged Celaeno. "Are you worried that you and the crew won't have any good luck, now that the garnet is staying here?"

"On the contrary, matey." Celaeno smirked. "We don't need a gem that's going to create riches or treasures for us. Us pirates think the adventure is the best part!" She leaned in to Rainbow Dash and spoke in a whisper. "Besides, now that we have friends like you, I think our true good fortune is just beginning." Captain Celaeno motioned her claw to the incredible scene in front of them. They had all made this possible, together. "What say you?"

"Aye!" Rainbow Dash could not agree more.

TURN THE PAGE FOR A SPECIAL LOOK AT

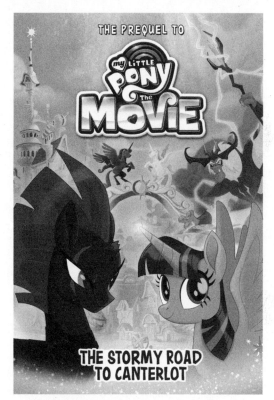

SEE HOW THE STORY BEGAN!

PROLOGUE

Tempest Shadow stood on the deck of the airship, looking down at Canterlot. The royal castle stood in the middle of the capital. She was hidden in the clouds high above. Nopony could see her. Nopony even knew she was there.

"It's an impressive city," she said, turning to Grubber. "But we have our chance. The Friendship Festival is happening soon."

"You think that would be a good time to steal the magic from the princesses?" Grubber asked. He sat next to her on the deck of the ship, talking in between bites of his muffin.

"The perfect time. We can descend from the airship to be safe," Tempest said. "There will be so many ponies in Canterlot during the festival, and everypony will be busy and having fun. We'll take them all by surprise."

"Genius plan," Grubber said.

"Now let's take one last look around. We should find out exactly where the entrance to the castle is, and what each of the princesses looks like. The more we know about Canterlot before the Friendship Festival, the better."

"But don't I need a disguise?" Grubber asked.

It felt like years since Tempest Shadow had met Grubber. The short, round creature was less than half her size, with a tuft of white hair and piercing blue eyes. She hadn't seen a creature like him before, in Equestria or anywhere else.

She grabbed two cloaks from the airship cabin and draped one over herself and one over Grubber. Then she ordered the ship down toward Canterlot. They'd dock on the outskirts of the city and make their way to the center. Who knew what they would find there...?

CHAPTER ONE

The young Unicorn walked through the forest, her two best friends right beside her. Glitter Drops and Spring Rain were Unicorns, too, and together the three of them liked to practice their magic. Every morning they'd venture out into the forest or explore the mountains by their small town, taking a break now and then to play ball.

"There it is," the young Unicorn said as they stepped into the clearing. She stared into the sky.

Canterlot was high above them. The capital of Equestria was perched in the mountains and could be seen for miles around. The three friends had never actually been there, but they'd heard hundreds of stories. The city was filled with ivory towers and waterfalls, shimmering spires and majestic views. Most important, it was the home of two of the three princesses, and a common spot for them to meet.

The three princesses were Alicorns, or Unicorns with powerful wings. Princess Celestia and Princess Luna controlled the sun and the moon, and Princess Cadance was the ruler of the Crystal Empire. She had been Princess Celestia's apprentice when she was younger.

"Do you think we'll ever get there?" Spring Rain asked.

"Of course we will," the young Unicorn said. "And who knows…"

Glitter Drops smiled. "Maybe one of us will become a princess one day, too."

"But first, Princess Celestia's School for Gifted Unicorns," the young Unicorn said. "Where all the most talented Unicorns learn to focus their powerful magic. We'll get there someday; I know we will."

The young Unicorn couldn't admit it to even her closest friends, but she thought about Princess Celestia's school every single day. She dreamed about studying in Canterlot, of learning to make magic that glowed and sparked with power. She'd work as hard as she could to make Princess Celestia proud. Sometimes she even imagined becoming an Alicorn herself. Would she ever be given wings? Could she ever be that powerful?

There were entrance exams every spring. The young Unicorn hoped she'd be ready when they came around one moon. She wanted to attend the school as soon as she could. It was hard waiting for something you wanted so much.

"Let's practice," she said, turning to Glitter Drops and Spring Rain. "Let's levitate the ball."

Glitter Drops's horn sparked and glowed. She took the ball from her satchel and sent it flying off into the woods. The young Unicorn darted after it, weaving in and out of the trees. She could just see the ball up ahead, glowing in the air. It was like the bouncy balls other ponies tossed back and forth, only this one was special. If she focused her magic, she could make it float and glow with a beautiful white light. It looked like the moon.

"I can't keep up!" Glitter Drops called out. She was running as fast as she could through the forest, but the ball was always a little ahead of her. She laughed as she ran, clearly loving the way the wind felt in her mane.

Spring Rain darted out in front of the young Unicorn. She raced across the ground to the ball, but she stumbled and fell. She hadn't been concentrating hard enough, but that wasn't her fault. It was tough to concentrate on her magic, run really fast, *and* keep her eyes on the ball.

The young Unicorn galloped out in front of both of her friends. The ball was up ahead.

She was so close. She just had to run a little faster....

"Where'd it go?" Spring Rain's voice called out. "It disappeared!"

The young Unicorn stopped at the mouth of a cave. The ball had floated inside. She could still see the glowing light, but it was dimmer now. The ball was somewhere in there, deep in the mountain.

"Oh no..." Glitter Drops stopped right behind her. She peered inside. The cave was so dark they couldn't see past the opening. "Who's going to go get it?"

Glitter Drops and Spring Rain turned to their brave friend. The purple Unicorn might've been the youngest, but she was always the bravest of the three. She'd talked to the hydra when they went to Froggy Bottom Bogg, and she had found her way through the Everfree Forest on her own. Whenever something scary happened, her friends always looked to her first.

"I'll be right back," the young Unicorn said. Then she ventured into the cave, trying to follow the dim light from the ball.

Inside, she could hardly see anything. The ball was somewhere up ahead, around a sharp corner, but she couldn't make out the floor of the cave. She stumbled over a rock and fell, landing hard. When she finally got up, her shoulder hurt.

"This isn't as easy as I thought it would be. . . ." she said to herself, rubbing the sore spot on her side. She went slower now, being careful with each step. "Just a little farther. . . ."

She was getting closer. As she turned the corner, she saw the ball floating in the air. That whole part of the cave was lit up now. She could see everything perfectly.

It looked like some creature had been living there. There were scraps of food and a warm, cozy bed. She reached up, grabbed the ball, and tucked it behind her front leg. When she turned back around, there was an ursa minor standing right in front of her.

She didn't have time to react. The bear roared in her face. She ducked underneath its foreleg, trying to get away, but it chased after her. She didn't move more than a few feet before it struck her with its giant paw. She went flying across the cave, her head knocking into the wall.

She got up as fast as she could, knowing the bear would be right behind her. As she got closer to the entrance of the cave, she could see Glitter Drops and Spring Rain waiting for her.

They were both staring inside the cave, trying to see what was happening.

"Run!" she yelled. "There's an ursa minor!"

Spring Rain and Glitter Drops turned around and darted off through the forest. The young Unicorn followed them, relieved when she was finally out of the cave. She'd dropped the ball at some point along the way, but it didn't matter. She had to get as far away from the ursa minor as she could.

She didn't stop running until she was out of the forest and saw Spring Rain and Glitter Drops standing in the field up ahead. She turned back, looking into the trees to make sure they were safe. After all that, they were finally alone. The bear hadn't followed them.

"I went all the way to the back of the cave," the young Unicorn said. "I found the ball, but then, when I turned around, the ursa minor was right behind me. It chased me, and then I fell, and then..."

Glitter Drops and Spring Rain just stared at her. Their eyes were wide, and their expressions were serious. They looked like something was horribly wrong. The young Unicorn glanced down at her hooves, making sure she wasn't hurt. She looked over her shoulder at her tail and mane. Everything seemed fine.

"I don't think I'm hurt," she said. "Just a few scratches..."

"I don't know how to tell you this...." Glitter Drops said, her eyes watering. "It's your horn."

The young Unicorn reached up and touched the front of her head. Her horn was just a small, jagged stump—the top half had broken off. Her eyes immediately filled with tears.

"No," she said, shaking her head. "No—it can't be. What's a Unicorn without her horn?"

"I'm so sorry." Glitter Drops hugged her friend.

"It'll be okay," Spring Rain added, wrapping her front leg around the young Unicorn's other side.

The tears streamed down the young Unicorn's cheeks. She'd lost her horn. All her magic was contained within it. How would anything ever be okay again?

CHAPTER TWO

The young Unicorn and her two friends set off through town, Spring Rain walking on one side of her and Glitter Drops walking on the other. She'd waited weeks, then months, for her horn to grow back, but nothing had happened. This was the first time she'd left her house since the day at the cave, but Spring Rain and Glitter Drops had told her it would be okay. She still couldn't help but feel nervous, though. Every time she looked at her broken horn she started crying.

She'd pulled a hat down over her head, and nopony seemed to notice anything was different. She waved at everypony inside the market, and everypony waved back. They passed their friend Moonglow, who was planting tulips outside the art gallery.

"What a lovely hat!" Moonglow said. "The flowers on it are beautiful."

"Thank you, Moonglow," the young Unicorn called as she trotted past.

"See?" Glitter Drops asked. "Is it really that bad?"

The young Unicorn shook her head. "You were right. It feels good to be out and about."

As they got to the clearing, Spring Rain looked around and took a ball out of her satchel.

There weren't many ponies near them. "Want to try it?" she asked. "It couldn't hurt...."

At first the young Unicorn wasn't sure what she was talking about. But then Spring Rain lifted the ball a few inches off the ground, levitating it in front of her.

"Oh, no...I shouldn't," the young Unicorn said. "I haven't used my horn for magic since the accident. I don't even know if it'll work."

"You're the bravest Unicorn we know," Glitter Drops said. "I always tell stories about my friend who isn't afraid of anypony or anything. You can do whatever you put your mind to."

The young Unicorn glanced back toward town. There wasn't anypony around. Maybe it wouldn't be the worst thing to just try. She hadn't had the courage to since her horn broke.

"Ready?" Spring Rain said, dropping the ball back to the ground.

The young Unicorn nodded and took off her hat. Glitter Drops and Spring Rain both trotted out in front of her, farther into the clearing. She focused her magic on her horn, trying to lift the ball off the ground. Her horn sparked. She stood there, waiting for it to work as a few more sparks shot out toward the trees.

Her power was building—she could feel it—and suddenly her broken horn shot off an incredible show of light. It was burning hot, and turned everything it touched to ash and dust. A whole row of trees burned underneath it.

"Watch out!" Glitter Drops cried as the young Unicorn stepped forward, trying to control it. She stumbled, and as her head turned, she scorched a patch of grass.

When her horn finally stopped shooting sparks, she stood there, trying to catch her breath. Spring Rain was lying in the grass. She'd bumped her head. Glitter Drops was hiding behind a tree. The young Unicorn reached out her hoof to help Spring Rain stand, but her friend flinched. When she stared up at her, her eyes were full of fear.

"I didn't mean it," the young Unicorn tried to explain. "I don't know what happened. . . ."

Spring Rain stood on her own. She brushed herself off and offered her friend a small smile. "It's okay. It was an accident."

Glitter Drops came up next to them, but the young Unicorn noticed both her friends didn't get too close. They kept glancing at her horn. They seemed afraid of her now. "Are you okay?" Glitter Drops asked Spring Rain. "That was a serious fall."

"I think I'm all right....It was just scary," Spring Rain said.

"I'm so sorry," the young Unicorn said. "It's something about my horn....It doesn't work right anymore."

"It's okay," Spring Rain said again, but she seemed sad. "Let's just go back home."

Glitter Drops and Spring Rain turned back toward town, and all the young Unicorn could do was follow. She knew Spring Rain was just frightened, but she couldn't help feeling like everything was her fault. Her horn was broken, her magic was gone, and things would never be the same between them. Everything had gone so wrong after that day at the cave.

She walked beside her friends, her hat snug on her head again. Glitter Drops and Spring

Rain didn't say anything else. The young Unicorn's mind was racing: Would she ever get her magic back? How would her friends be able to trust her? And how could she stay in her town when everything felt so wrong?

CHAPTER THREE

The moons passed. The young Unicorn spent more and more time at home, reading and baking and doing anything that didn't remind her of the magic she'd once had. Glitter Drops and Spring Rain still came by to see her every once in a while, but they never asked her to go to the clearing with them to practice magic. They never even mentioned her horn. Instead they pretended as if that day in the cave had never happened.

So when they knocked on her door one morning, she hoped maybe something had changed. Maybe they weren't afraid of her after all.

She flung open the door.

"Where to?" she asked. She'd already put on her hat. It had been so long since she'd seen her friends; she couldn't help but miss them and all the fun times they'd had. She'd just go with them to get some apple cider, and then she'd come home. She wouldn't even talk about magic or what they used to do in the clearing.

"Actually..." Glitter Drops began slowly. She looked a little sad. "We wanted to talk to you about something."

"What do you mean?" the young Unicorn asked.

"We took the entrance exams for Princess Celestia's School for Gifted Unicorns," Spring Rain said. "We wanted to tell you before you heard it from any other pony."

The young Unicorn tried to hide the hurt in her expression, but she could already feel her eyes welling up with tears. Since the day she'd broken her horn, she'd tried to bury her dreams down deep in her heart. She hoped that one day her horn would grow back, along with her magic, and she could go to Princess Celestia's school, but until then she tried her best to forget. Sometimes she wouldn't even glance up at Canterlot. It was hard to see the city glittering in the sky and not think of all the possibilities of a future there.

"I didn't realize they'd happened already," the young Unicorn said. "I just...I hadn't thought about it since..."

"We know," Glitter Drops said. "And we know your horn is going to grow back soon. It's only a matter of time. But we felt like we had to take the exams this moon. The term starts in the fall."

"So you're going?" she asked as she tried to steady her voice.

"Yeah," Spring Rain said. "But you'll come next moon. We'll all be together again soon. And we'll come back to visit all the time. We'll still be friends."

"Right," the young Unicorn said. "Of course. We'll always be friends. I'm happy for you."

The young Unicorn put on her best smile, even though she was hurting. Glitter Drops and Spring Rain looked relieved that she was being so nice about it. She said good-bye to her friends, and they promised that they'd see one another the next day. She told them they were going to have the best time at Princess Celestia's school. Then she closed the door and started to cry.

+ + ⧙⧘ + +

The young Unicorn put on the cloak she had pieced together and stared at the bag on the floor. She pulled it onto her back, knowing she had no other choice. If she stayed, she'd always be different. The Unicorn with the broken horn. The Unicorn without magic. The Unicorn whose friends left her behind. What kind of life would that be?

She stepped outside, pulled up her hood, and turned back one last time to say good-bye to her cottage. She'd leave tonight, for good. There were other places she could go, and other ponies who might accept her. She couldn't keep pretending she was happy here. This town no longer felt like home.

As she started off into the night, she reminded herself of the worst part. She'd been the brave one that day in the forest. She'd volunteered to go into the cave to get the ball so her friends didn't have to. She'd yelled to Glitter Drops and Spring Rain, telling them there was an ursa minor inside so they wouldn't get hurt. She'd done everything right.

And what did she have to show for it? What did she get for being a good friend?

Nothing, she thought as the lights from the town grew smaller in the distance. *There's nothing left for me there.*